7133 .

47½p

D1439152

Don Gress

THE NEW WINDMILL SERIES

General Editors: Anne and Ian Serraillier

113

Night Flight

Based on the author's own experiences when he was sent to South America to help establish commercial air-lines to Europe, this is a dramatic story of the risks and dangers of night-flying in its early days. The author, a first-rate story-teller with a rare poetic imagination, writes with warm feeling and conviction, and is able to suggest a deeper significance behind the objects and the situations portrayed. A classic of its kind, the book will be enjoyed by boys interested in stories of flying, while many girls will appreciate its rich emotional appeal.

Antoine de Saint-Exupéry

NIGHT FLIGHT

translated from the French by

CURTIS CATE

*(with acknowledgements to
Stuart Gilbert's translations)*

HEINEMANN EDUCATIONAL
BOOKS LIMITED · LONDON

Heinemann Educational Books Ltd

LONDON   EDINBURGH   MELBOURNE   TORONTO
SINGAPORE   JOHANNESBURG   HONG KONG
NAIROBI   AUCKLAND   IBADAN   NEW DELHI

ISBN O 435 12113 8

Vol de Nuit, first published 1931 (Gallimard)
Night Flight, translation by Stuart Gilbert, 1932
(Crosby Continental Editions)
retranslated by Curtis Cate, 1971 (Heinemann)

Night Flight revised translation
© William Heinemann Ltd, 1971
First published in the New Windmill Series 1971

FRONTISPIECE
A Laté 28
reproduced by kind permission of
Air France

Published by
Heinemann Educational Books Ltd
48 Charles Street, London W1X 8AH

Printed in Great Britain by
Morrison and Gibb Ltd, London and Edinburgh

Preface

ANTOINE DE SAINT-EXUPÉRY, French novelist and pioneer airman, was born in Lyons on June 29th, 1900. He lost his father when he was four. A strong and active child with an inventive turn of mind, he was already at six years old writing poetry. He would wake his younger brother and three sisters in the night to read it to them. At the Jesuit College of Notre Dame de Sainte Croix at Le Mans it was linguistic work that interested him most, and other school subjects not at all. Yet during the first World War, when he was at school in Paris preparing to enter the Navy, he failed in the oral and got a poor mark in the essay.

During his military service (1921-3) he took up flying. His first lessons were with a civilian air pilot, who was stingy with his petrol. One day, impatient to launch out on his own, with a total of less than an hour's instruction in the air, he took off solo. The plane started to catch fire, and he was lucky to land without disaster. Later, just before his demobilization, he was less fortunate. While landing at Le Bourget, he fractured his skull. This was the first of several severe accidents, none of which ever put him off flying.

In 1926 he got a job carrying air-mail between Toulouse and Dakar. After a few months of this, he was put in charge of a calling station on the North African coast. It was here that he wrote his first novel, *Southern Mail*, a romanticized novel based on his own experiences, about an air-mail pilot in West Africa.

In 1929 he was sent to Buenos Aires to set up a mail service along the coast of Patagonia as far south as the Straits of Magellan. The region was notorious for cyclones and hurricanes, and the establishment of a night service was a particularly risky undertaking. On his experiences as flight director here St Exupéry based his second novel, *Night Flight*. The book shows what it cost in human suffering and loss of life to found a new and vital tradition. The cyclone in which the pilot Fabien is caught was one which St Exupéry himself had once to struggle with on this very route, and the fate to which Fabien eventually succumbs is modelled on a tragic accident that befell two of the author's companions in 1930.

Also modelled from life is the novel's central character, Rivière, the pilots' iron leader. He is a man with strong human feelings and a tender concern for his pilots, but he will allow nothing to stand in the way of a meticulous attention to duty. Rivière, as André Gide has written, "does not act himself; he prods others into action, imbuing his pilots with his own virtues, exacting the utmost out of them, and forcing them to deeds of prowess. His implacable determination tolerates no flinching, and the slightest lapse is punished by him. His severity might at first sight seem inhuman and excessive. But it is to his imperfections that it applies, and not to the man himself, whom Rivière seeks to mould. In his portrayal of him we sense the fullness of the author's admiration.

"I am particularly grateful to him for bringing out a paradoxical truth which seems to me of considerable psychological importance: that man's happiness lies not in freedom but in the acceptance of a duty." This truth is in fact the central theme of the book. Each character is devoted to it and finds fulfilment in dedication to a task larger than himself, to something to which "he subordinates and sacrifices himself".

Concisely and dramatically told by a story-teller of remarkable skill, the novel is much more than a tale of adventure. In its philosophical and poetic approach to its subject, it is distinctively French. St Exupéry's style has in it something of the beauty of Gide's prose. There are magnificent descriptions of storms and blizzards, of what it feels like to be flying through clouds; a sense too of the immensity of the skies and the smallness of the earth-planet as it circles in the universe. Above all, the novel conveys the feeling of wonder inspired in the airman during the heroic age of the pioneers. St Exupéry was to write other books, but *Night Flight* was his masterpiece and established his reputation. He was in Paris for its publication in 1931.

The rest of his career can be quickly told. In 1933, while working as a test pilot, he narrowly escaped drowning in the Bay of St Raphael. Two years later, during an attempt at a record-breaking flight from Paris to Saigon, he crashed in the African desert. *Terre des Hommes* (1939) tells the story of this flight and how he and his mechanic nearly died of thirst before they were rescued by an Arab. When in 1938 he was trying to reconnoitre a route from New York to Tierra del Fuego, he crashed in Guatemala and was severely injured. His enthusiasm for adventure survived several operations and a long convalescence.

On the outbreak of war in 1939 he served first as a navigational instructor, then (in spite of his age) as a reconnaissance pilot yet again. After taking a heroic part in the Battle of France in 1940, he spent two years in New York, writing. *Letter to a Hostage*, *Flight to Arras*, which describes the collapse of France and was prompted by the need for fresh vision and initiative, and *The Little Prince*, a fairy-tale and allegory for children, illustrated by the author's own water-colours, all belong to this period. In the spring of 1943 he went with an American convoy to North Africa, where he reorganized his old flying group and, after a minor landing accident, was put on the reserve list. This was hardly to his liking. Somehow he got the decision changed and soon found himself back doing reconnaissance flights. From the ninth of these—on July 31st, 1944—he never returned. It is thought that a German fighter shot him down.

Ian Serraillier

Sources:

Vol de Nuit, Antoine de St-Exupéry, ed. by F. A. Shuffrey, M.C., M.A., William Heinemann, 1952
Preface to *Night Flight*, André Gide, translated by Curtis Cate, William Heinemann, 1971
The Penguin Companion to Literature, vol. 2, European, ed. by A. K. Thorlby

I

ALREADY, beneath him, the shadowed hills had dug their furrows in the golden evening and the plains grown luminous with long-enduring light. For in these lands the ground is slow to yield its sunset gold, just as in the waning winter the whiteness of the snow persists.

Fabien, the pilot who was flying the Patagonia mail from the extreme south to Buenos Aires, could note the onset of night by the same tell-tale signs as a harbour: by the calm expanse before him, faintly rippled by lazy clouds. He was entering a vast and happy anchorage.

In this calm he could also have fancied himself, like a shepherd, going for a quiet walk. Thus the shepherds of Patagonia move unhurriedly from one flock to another. He was moving from one city to the next, and the little towns were his sheep. Every two hours he came upon one slaking its thirst by the riverside or browsing off its plain.

Sometimes, after sixty miles of steppes as uninhabited as the sea, he came upon a lonely farm, which seemed to bob backward on its billow of prairie lands, carrying away its cargo of human lives; he then dipped his wings, as though saluting a ship.

*

"San Julián in sight. We'll be landing in ten minutes."

The radio operator on board transmitted the news to all the airfields of the network. From the Straits of Magellan to Buenos Aires similar airstrips were strung out over more than fifteen hundred miles. But this one was located on the borderland of night —much as in Africa the last conquered hamlet opens on to the unknown.

The radio operator passed up a slip of paper to the pilot. "There are so many thunderstorms around that my earphones are full of static. Shall we stop the night at San Julián?"

Fabien smiled. The sky was as calm as an aquarium, and all the airfields ahead of them were signalling: "Clear sky, no wind."

"We'll go on," he replied.

Somewhere, the radio operator thought, a few thunderstorms had managed to lodge themselves, like worms inside a piece of fruit. The night would be beautiful yet spoiled, and he felt ill at ease at the thought of entering this shadow that was ripe to rottenness.

*

Fabien felt tired, as he came down towards San Julián, his engine idling. Looming up to meet him came everything that softens the life of men—their houses, their little cafés, the trees lining their promenades. He was like a conqueror in the aftermath of victory who broods over the lands of his empire and discovers the humble happiness of his subjects. Fabien felt the need to lay down his arms, to feel out his heavy aches and cramps—for one is rich also in one's discomforts—and to become here a simple human being able to look out of the window at an unchanging scene. He would gladly have accepted this tiny village. The choice once made, one can content oneself with the hazard of one's existence and learn to love it. Like love, it hems you in. Fabien would have liked to settle down here, enjoying his morsel of eternity; for the little towns in which he tarried but an hour, and the closed gardens behind old walls over which he flew, seemed to him eternal —for lasting independently of him.

The little town now rose towards the plane, opening wide its arms. Fabien thought of all the friendships it contained, the gentle girls, the privacy of white table-cloths, of everything that is slowly domesticated for eternity. Already the village was streaking past his wings, unfolding the mystery of sheltered gardens no longer shielded by their walls. Yet Fabien knew, even as he landed, that he had seen nothing save a few slow men moving quietly among their stones. By virtue of its very immobility this village defended the secrecy of its passions, withheld its soft welcome; and to conquer it he would have had to give up action.

*

When the ten-minute stop-over was ended, Fabien resumed his flight. He turned to look back at San Julián, now a mere handful of lights. The lights became stars, then a twinkling dust which faded into nothingness along with its temptations.

*

"I can no longer see the dials: I'll light up."

He flicked on the switches, but the red cockpit lamps gave off a glow that was still so pale in the blue light that it scarcely coloured the needles. He passed his fingers in front of a bulb, but they were barely reddened.

Yet the night was rising, like a dark smoke, and already filling the valleys, which could no longer be distinguished from the plains. The villages were lighting up, greeting each other across the dusk like constellations. With a flick of his finger he blinked his wing-lights in answer. The earth was now dotted with luminous appeals, each house now lighting up its star against the immensity of the night, much as a beacon is trained upon the sea. Everything that sheltered human life now sparkled; and Fabien was overjoyed that his entry into the night should this time be slow and beautiful, like an entry into port.

He ducked his head down inside the cockpit. The phosphorescent needles had begun to glow. One after the other he checked the figures and was happy. He felt himself solidly ensconced in this evening sky. He ran a finger along a steel rib and felt the life coursing through it; the metal was not vibrant but alive. The engine's five hundred horse-power had charged the matter with a gentle current, changing its icy deadness into velvet flesh. Once again the pilot in flight experienced neither giddiness nor intoxicating thrill, but only the mysterious travail of living flesh.

He had made a world for himself once more. He moved his arms to feel even more at home, then ran his thumb over the electric circuit diagram. He fingered the various switches, shifted his weight, settled back, and sought to find the position best suited for feeling the oscillations of these five tons of metal which a moving night had shouldered. Groping with his fingers, he pushed the emergency lamp into position, let it go, seized hold of it again after making sure it wouldn't slip, then let go to touch each throttle lever and to assure himself that he could reach them without looking—thus training his fingers for a blind man's world. His fingers having taken stock of everything, he switched on a lamp, decking out his cockpit with precision instruments. Attentive to the dial readings, he could now enter the night, like a submarine starting on its dive. There was no trembling, no shaking, no undue vibration; and as his gyroscope, altimeter, and r.p.m. rate remained constant, he stretched his limbs, leaned his head back against the leather seat, and fell into an airborne meditation rich with unfathomable hopes.

*

Now, swallowed up by the night like a watchman, he could see how the night betrays man's secrets: those appeals, those lights, that anxiety. That single star down there in the shadow—a house in isolation. That other star flickering and going out—a house closing the shutters on its love. Or on its boredom. A house that has ceased signalling to the rest of the world. Gathered around their lamp-lit table, those farmers little guessed the true measure of their hopes nor realized how far their yearnings reached in the great night that encompassed them. But Fabien, approaching from six hundred miles away, uncovered them along with the ground-swells that lifted and lowered his breathing plane. Having traversed ten storms, like battlefields, and the moon-lit clearings between them, he now picked up these lights, one after another, with a pride of conquest. Down there they thought their lamp was lit for their humble table, but already from fifty miles away one was touched by its desolate appeal, as though they were desperately swinging it, from a deserted island, at the dark immensity of the sea.

II

From south, west, and north the three mail-planes from Patagonia, Chile, and Paraguay were now converging on Buenos Aires. Here their mail-loads were awaited, prior to the departure, around midnight, of the Europe-bound plane.

Three pilots, each behind a cowling as heavy as a river-barge, were thus lost in the night. Wrapped in their airborne meditations, they would soon, from their skies of storm or calm, begin their slow descent towards the great city, like rough backwoodsmen descending from their mountains.

On the landing field of Buenos Aires Rivière, who was responsible for the entire network, was pacing up and down. He said nothing, for until the three planes were safely landed, this day for him remained fraught with anxiety. With each passing minute, as the telegrams came in, Rivière felt he was wrenching something from blind fate, he was reducing the area of uncertainty, and pulling his crews out of the night and towards the shore.

A member of the ground crew came up to him with a message from the radio hut:

"Chile mail-plane reports Buenos Aires lights in sight."

"Fine."

Rivière would soon hear its welcome drone. Already the night was yielding up one of its prey—much as the sea, in the ebb and flow of its mysterious currents, deposits on the shore a treasure it has long tossed about. Later he would retrieve the other two. Then his work-day would be finished. Then the exhausted crews could go to bed, replaced by a new shift. Rivière alone would know no rest; for the Europe-bound mail-plane would cause him anxieties in its turn. So it would always be. Always.

For the first time this veteran battler experienced

a surprising lassitude. Never could his planes' arrival bring him that victory which terminates a war and opens an era of joyous peace. Each forward step he took would be followed by a thousand others like it, remaining to be taken. He was oppressed by the numbing weight of this burden he had been carrying, with taut arms, for so long: it was an effort without hope of respite.

"I must be ageing," he thought. Yes, ageing—if he could no longer find solace in his work. He was surprised to find himself turning over questions he had never stopped to ask—above the melancholic murmur of gentle joys he had consistently pushed aside, like an unsailed ocean. "Is it then so near?" For years, he realized, he had been postponing for his old age, for "when I have time for it", everything that softens and sweetens human life. As though one day one really could find the time, as though at the very extremity of one's life one could gain the blessed peace one had imagined. But there was no peace; perhaps not even victory. There was no such thing as a definitive arrival for every mail-plane in the air.

Rivière stopped in front of Leroux, an old foreman who was hard at work. Leroux, too, had been working forty years; a work that had consumed all his strength. When Leroux went home at ten o'clock or midnight, it was not another world that greeted him, it was not an evasion. Rivière smiled, as the man raised his heavy head and pointed to a polished axle: "The fit was too tight, but I've pared her down a bit."

Rivière bent down to peer at the steel-blue axle. His work once again absorbed him.

"We must tell the workshops to adjust these pieces more loosely." He ran his finger over the area which had seized, then looked at Leroux again. At the sight of those stern wrinkles a strange question rose to his lips and made him smile.

"In your life, Leroux, have you ever been much concerned with love?"

"Love, Monsieur le Directeur! . . . Huh . . ."

"Like me, you've never had time for it."

"No, not much . . ."

Rivière listened to his voice, seeking to detect a note of bitterness in the reply. But there was none. Looking back over his life, this man experienced the quiet contentment of the carpenter who has just polished a handsome board. "There, it's done."

"That's it," thought Rivière. "My life is done."

Brushing aside the sombre thoughts his fatigue had brought on, he walked towards the hangar; for already he could hear the drone of the plane from Chile.

III

The sound of the distant engine grew steadily denser: a sound that was ripening. The lights were switched on. The red markers winked gaily from the hangar roof, hung like rubies from the radio aerials, and traced out a rectangle on the ground. A gala fiesta!

"Here she comes!"

The plane rolled towards them, already caught in a cross-fire of beams which made it sparkle like a fish. Halted at last in front of the hangar, mechanics and ground crewmen crowded round to unload the mail, but the pilot, Pellerin, did not move.

"Well, and what are you waiting for?"

The pilot, busy with some mysterious task, did not bother to reply. Probably his ears were still full of the noise of the flight. He nodded his head deliberately as he leaned forward to tinker with some unseen object. Finally he turned towards the officials and the crewmen and looked them over gravely, as though they belonged to him. He seemed to be counting, measuring, and weighing them; he had earned them well, he thought, like this festooned hangar and this solid strip of cement, and farther on, the city with its bustle, its women, and its warmth. He held these people in his broad hands, like subjects, since he could touch them, hear them, insult them. For a moment he felt like bawling them out for standing there so quietly, so unimperilled, so full of gaping admiration for the moon; but instead he greeted them nonchalantly:

". . . Owe me a drink!"

And he climbed down. He wanted to tell them of his flight:

"If only you knew . . ."

But evidently deciding that he had said enough, he walked off to change out of his leather gear.

*

As the chauffeur-driven roadster took him into Buenos Aires, seated next to a taciturn Rivière and a morose inspector, Pellerin suddenly felt dejected. It was fine to pull through like this and to let go with a volley of swearwords as one set foot on solid ground. It made one feel great! But later, when one looked back on it, one began to wonder . . .

That struggle with the blizzard, that at least was real, straightforward. But not the curious look things have when they think they are alone. "It's like a mutiny," he thought. "The faces are only a wee shade paler, but everything's completely changed."

He made an effort to recall the precise sequence of events. He had been flying over the cordillera of the Andes. Beneath their coverlets of snow the mountains slept. The winter snows had spread their peace over this mountain mass, like the passage of the centuries in dead castles. One hundred and twenty miles across, one hundred and twenty miles of thickness—without a man, a breath of life, a movement. Nothing but vertical ridges which one grazed at twenty thousand feet, nothing but gigantic coats of stone dropping sheer, nothing but an awe-inspiring silence.

Then, as he was approaching the peak of

Tupungato—he paused—yes, it was there that he had witnessed a miracle.

At first he had noticed nothing, but simply experienced a vague malaise—such as a man feels when, thinking himself alone, he suddenly becomes aware that someone is watching him. Too late and without understanding why, he felt himself ringed by anger. That was all. Yet why this feeling? By what tell-tale sign could he sense it oozing from the rocks, oozing from the snow? For nothing seemed on its way to meet him, no sombre storm was on the march. Yet a different world, so faintly different as to be barely perceptible, was right here emerging from the other. Pellerin looked on with an inexplicable tightening of the heart—at these innocent peaks, those snowy crests which, grown only slightly greyer, were now beginning to live—like a people.

Instinctively his hands tightened their grip on the controls. Something he did not understand was brewing. He steeled his muscles, like a beast about to spring, but there was nothing he could see that wasn't calm. Calm, yes, but charged with a weird power.

Suddenly everything began to sharpen. Crests, peaks grew razor sharp, cutting into the hard wind like bowsprits. And it seemed to him that they were veering and drifting like giant dreadnoughts, taking up their battle stations around him. Then, faintly mingled with the air, came a fine dust which rose, floating softly like a veil, along the snow. He glanced back, to see if, in case of need, there was an avenue of escape behind him, and shuddered: the entire cordillera behind him was now in seething ferment.

"I'm done for!"

From a peak dead ahead of him the snow suddenly flared—the fume of a white volcano. Then from a second peak, slightly to the right. One after another, all the peaks caught fire as though successively touched by some invisible runner. And now, as the first air bumps hit him, the mountains about him began to dance.

Violent action leaves little trace behind it; and of the mighty buffeting which followed he had but a dim recollection. All he could remember was how grimly he had fought it out in the midst of those grey flames.

"A blizzard," he reflected, "is nothing. One saves one's skin. But just before—that weird encounter!"

That changing face, that one face in a thousand he was sure he could recognize ... had fled, and he could no longer say what it was like.

IV

Rivière looked at the pilot. When in twenty minutes' time Pellerin climbed out of the car, he would lose himself in the crowd with a feeling of heavy-limbed fatigue. "I'm worn out ... What a dog's life!" he might think. To his wife he might admit that "one's a lot better off here than over the Andes!" Yet everything men cling to most dearly had almost been ripped from him; he had sensed its fragility. He had just lived through several hours behind the *trompe-l'oeil* screen of this deceptive world, without knowing if he would be allowed to regain this city with its lights, if he would be allowed to renew acquaintance with those irksome but dear companions of his youth, his all too human frailties.

"In every crowd," Rivière thought, "there are people whom one cannot tell from the rest but who are prodigious messengers. Without their realizing it themselves . . . Unless . . ."

Rivière was wary of certain admirers, those who do not understand the sacred character of adventure, whose enthusiastic exclamations distort its meaning and debase the individual. Pellerin's merit lay in his knowing, better than anyone, what the world is like when it has been glimpsed in a certain light, and in repelling all vulgar displays of approval with a weary disdain. Rivière therefore congratulated him quite simply: "But how did you manage it?" Liking him all the more for talking shop, for speaking of his flight as a blacksmith speaks of his anvil.

Pellerin began by explaining that his retreat was cut off. He almost apologized for it. "I was thus left with no choice." Then everything had been swallowed up, and he had been completely blinded by the snow. He had been saved by some violent updraughts which had lifted him to twenty-two thousand feet. "I must have been carried straight over the peaks for the entire crossing." He also spoke of the gyroscope, saying that the position of its air-intake should be altered: the snow clogged it up—"It frosts up, you see." Later he had been tossed around by other air currents, and Pellerin did not understand how he could have dropped to ten thousand feet without smashing into something. In reality, he was already flying over the plain. "I didn't realize it until I suddenly came out into a clear sky." At which point he had had the impression of emerging from a cave.

"Was it stormy at Mendoza too?"

"No. I landed under a clear sky, and there was no wind. But the storm was hot on my heels."

He described it because, as he said, "it was a bit odd, after all." The top of the storm was lost high up in the snow clouds, while at its base it rolled out over the plain like black lava. One by one it had blotted out the towns. "Never seen anything like it . . ." He lapsed into silence, gripped by some memory.

Rivière turned to the inspector.

"It's a cyclone from the Pacific, they failed to warn us in time. Anyway, these cyclones never get beyond the Andes."

The inspector, who knew nothing, agreed—little realizing that contrary to all expectations, this one would carry on towards the east.

*

The inspector seemed to hesitate, turned towards Pellerin, and his Adam's apple moved. But he said nothing, preferring on second thoughts to look

23

straight ahead of him and retain his melancholy dignity.

He had been carrying this melancholy around like a handbag. He had landed the evening before in Argentina, summoned by Rivière on some unspecified assignment; but he felt encumbered as much by his big hands as by his inspectorial dignity. He had no right to admire fantasy or verve; it was his job to admire punctuality. He had no right to have a drink with the others, to call a pilot by his first name, or to risk a pun unless, by some extraordinary coincidence, he happened to bump into another inspector at the same airfield.

"It's difficult," he thought, "to be a judge."

In sober fact he didn't judge, he merely nodded his head. To mask his ignorance, he nodded his head deliberately, whatever came his way. It troubled the consciences of those who had reasons for feeling guilty, and it contributed to the good upkeep of the material. He was not liked, for inspectors are not created for the delights of love but for the drafting of reports. He had given up proposing new methods and technical solutions since the day Rivière had written: "Inspector Robineau is requested to supply us with reports, not poems. Inspector Robineau will put his talents to good use by stimulating the zeal of the personnel." Since then he had fastened on human failings as on his daily bread—the mechanic with a fondness for the bottle, the airfield boss who lived it up at night, the pilot who bounced his plane on landing.

Rivière liked to say of him: "He's not very intelligent, which is why he gives us yeoman service." A regulation laid down by Rivière afforded him a knowledge of his men; but for Robineau what mattered was a knowledge of the regulations.

"Robineau," Rivière had said to him one day, "for all tardy take-offs you must cancel the punctuality bonus."

"Even when it's no one's fault? Even in case of fog?"

"Even in case of fog."

Robineau had felt a kind of pride in having a boss who was not afraid to be unjust. Robineau even derived a certain majesty from such an uncompromising power.

"You had the plane take off at 6.15," he would later repeat to the airfield controllers, "we can't pay you your bonus."

"But Monsieur Robineau, at 5.30 one couldn't see ten yards in front of one."

"Those are the regulations."

"But Monsieur Robineau, we can't sweep the fog away!"

Robineau withdrew into his mystery. He was part of the management. He alone, among all these nonentities, understood how, in punishing individuals, one improves the weather.

"He doesn't think," Rivière used to say of him, "which keeps him from thinking wrong."

If a pilot damaged a plane, he lost his no-accident bonus.

"And what if his motor gives out over a wood?" Robineau had asked.

"He still loses it over a wood."

Robineau did not try to argue.

"I regret," he would later say to the pilots, almost zestfully. "I even regret it greatly, but you should have had your breakdown somewhere else."

"But Monsieur Robineau, one can't choose . . ."

"Those are the regulations."

"Regulations," thought Rivière, "are like the rites of a religion which seem absurd but which mould men." Rivière did not mind whether he appeared just or unjust. Perhaps these words were devoid of meaning for him. The *petit bourgeois* inhabitants of little provincial towns go strolling in the evening around their bandstands, and Rivière thought: "Being fair or unfair towards them is meaningless; they don't exist." Man for him was like a lump of wax waiting to be moulded. It was up to him to give a soul to this matter, to imbue it with a will. In bearing down he had no thought of enslaving them; he meant to raise them up above themselves. In punishing for each delay he might be unjust, but on every airfield he was galvanizing a will to punctuality, and thus creating this will. Denying his men a chance to rejoice over cloudy weather, as a pretext for indolence, he kept them on the qui vive for the first break, and even the humblest groundcrew worker felt secretly humiliated by the delay. Thus they learned to take advantage of the first chink in the armour. "There's a break in the north. Be off!" Thanks to Rivière, the cult of the mail took precedence over everything—over a distance of ten thousand miles.

Occasionally Rivière would say: "These men are happy because they enjoy what they're doing, and they enjoy it because I'm tough."

Perhaps he made men suffer, but he also afforded them keen joys. "They must be pushed," he thought, "towards a hardy life involving suffering and joy which by itself matters infinitely more."

As the automobile entered the city, Rivière had himself driven to the Company offices. Robineau, finding himself alone with Pellerin, looked at him and opened his mouth to speak.

V

Now Robineau this evening felt downcast. In contrast to Pellerin the winner, he was made painfully aware of what a grey life was his. Above all, it dawned on him that for all his authority and title of Inspector, he, Robineau, counted for less than this weary fellow who now sat slumped back in one corner of the car with his eyes closed and his hands black with oil. For the first time Robineau was seized with a genuine admiration. He felt the need to say so, and particularly needed to make a friend. His own trip had tired him and the day's rebuffs perhaps made him feel a bit ridiculous. A bare hour or two before he had got mixed up in his figures while checking the fuel stocks, and the very agent he had hoped to catch off guard had finally taken pity and finished them for him. Worse still, he had criticized the installation of a B6 type oil-pump, confusing it with a B4 type oil-pump, and the mechanics had slyly let him rant on for twenty minutes against "an ignorance for which there's no excuse" and which was quite simply his own.

He also dreaded his hotel room. From Toulouse to Buenos Aires it was inevitably to it that he repaired when the day's work was done. He would close the door behind him, conscious of the secrets to which he had been privy, and pulling out a sheaf of paper from his suitcase, he would begin with deliberate care: "Report", try out a couple of lines, and then tear everything up. He would have liked to rescue the Company from some mighty peril, but it was not in danger. All he had so far rescued was a propeller-boss, slightly touched by rust. He had slowly run his finger over this rust with a rueful air, in the presence of the airfield controller, whose only comment was: "Take it up with the previous stop. This plane's only just come in."

Robineau was losing confidence in his rôle.

To win Pellerin over he hazarded an invitation: "Would you like to have dinner with me? I could do with a little conversation, and my job's sometimes tiring . . ." But to keep his dignity from slipping too far, he hastily rectified: "I've so many responsibilities."

His subordinates didn't care to bring Robineau

28

into their private lives. Each thought to himself: "If he hasn't yet dug up something for his report, he'll dig his teeth into me."

But Robineau this evening could think only of his physical afflictions: the annoying eczema which plagued his body, his one and only secret, a secret he would have liked to share, to elicit sympathy; for the solace he could not find in pride he was ready to look for in humility. And then there was the mistress, back in France, whom he would regale with descriptions of his inspection tours each time he came home. He thus hoped to dazzle her a little and make her love him, but all it did was get on her nerves. About her too he felt the need to talk.

"Well, will you dine with me?"

Good-naturedly Pellerin accepted.

VI

The secretaries were drowsing in the Buenos Aires offices when Rivière walked in. He had kept on his overcoat and hat, like the eternal traveller he always seemed to be. So spare was he of build and so perfectly did his grey hair and suit adapt themselves to different settings that his presence went almost unperceived. However, a sudden zeal seized hold of the staff. The secretaries began bustling about, the chief clerk leafed hurriedly through the latest papers, the typewriters began to click.

The switchboard operator kept plugging in his

leads, jotting down the telegrams in a bulky register. Rivière sat down and read them. The Chile mail-plane's ordeal now over, they recorded one of those uneventful days when everything goes smoothly and each new airfield message is like a victory bulletin. The Patagonia mail-plane was also doing well; it was even ahead of schedule, for the southern winds were pushing it northwards on their mighty tide.

"Hand me the weather reports."

Each airfield vaunted its fine weather, its transparent sky, its friendly breeze. A golden evening now robed America. Rivière was pleased to find things going so well. Somewhere this mail-plane was now at grips with the perils of the night, but the odds were in its favour.

"All right," said Rivière, laying down the register.

And he walked out, tireless watchman of the hemisphere, to have a look at what the rest of his staff were doing.

*

He stopped before an open window and gazed out at the night. It contained Buenos Aires, but also, like some huge hull, America. This feeling of immensity did not surprise him. The sky of Santiago de Chile might be a foreign sky, but once the mail-plane was off for Santiago, from one end of the line to the other one lived under the same deep vault. The fishermen of Patagonia could now see the navigation lights of the mail-plane whose message the radio operators were straining to catch in their earphones. The anxiety that preyed upon Rivière when a plane was in flight was the same as that which weighed upon the capitals and provinces, disturbed by an engine's restless drone.

Relieved by this auspicious night, he recalled nights of chaos and confusion, when the plane had seemed dangerously beset and so difficult to succour. Its plaintive calls were received at the Buenos Aires radio hut amid the atmospheric cracklings of thunderstorms. Beneath this sonic landslide the golden vein of the wave-length disappeared. What piercing distress in this plaintive minor key of a mail-plane launched like a blind arrow at night's obstacles!

*

It occurred to Rivière that an inspector's place, when the staff is on night duty, is in the office.

"Send for Robineau," he said.

Robineau, in his hotel room, was in the process of making a friend of the pilot. He had opened his suitcase in front of him and dragged out a few trivial belongings whereby inspectors prove their kinship with the rest of mankind: some deplorably-styled shirts, a toilet kit, and a woman's photograph which the inspector pinned up on the wall. To Pellerin he thus made the humble confession of his needs, affections, and regrets. A pitiful hoard of treasures which he laid out before the pilot as a token of his wretchedness. It was a moral eczema, a prison which he thus unveiled.

But for Robineau, as for all men, there was a crack in the darkness. And it was with something akin to rapture that he pulled up from the bottom of his suitcase a small, preciously wrapped bag. He fondled it for a long moment without a word. Then removing his hands, he said:

"I brought these back from the Sahara."

The inspector, in hazarding this confession, blushed. In these blackish pebbles which opened a door on a mysterious world, he had found solace from his setbacks and sentimental misadventures and the grey drudgery of his life.

Blushing even deeper, he added: "One can find the same in Brazil."

Amused by the sight of this inspector, who nourished his own mystery of Atlantis, Pellerin gave him a friendly pat on the back, before dutifully inquiring:

"You like geology?"

"I'm mad about it."

Stones, in his harsh existence, were the only soft things he had ever known.

*

Informed that he was wanted at the office, Robineau felt sad but promptly resumed his dignity.

"I must leave you. Monsieur Rivière needs my assistance for some important decisions."

When Robineau walked into the office, Rivière

had forgotten all about him. He was staring wonderingly at a wall-map on which the Company's network had been traced out in red. The inspector stood waiting for his orders. Finally, after several long minutes, Rivière addressed him, without turning his head.

"What do you think of this map, Robineau?"

Often Rivière would interrupt his meditations by springing a conundrum on his startled visitor.

"That map, Monsieur le Directeur . . ."

The inspector, in reality, had no ideas on the subject. But now, focusing on it with a frown, he inspected the land masses of Europe and America. Rivière, meanwhile, was pursuing his own silent train of thought. "The outline of this network is beautiful but hard. It's cost us a lot of men, young men too. Here it imposes itself with the self-evidence of a finished structure, but what a host of problems it presents!" For Rivière, however, the goal took precedence over everything.

Robineau, who had been standing beside him looking fixedly at the map, gradually drew himself up. From Rivière, he knew he could expect no pity. He had once made a fumbling effort to obtain it by avowing his physical infirmities, and Rivière had answered with a quip: "If it keeps you from sleeping, it should stimulate your activity."

Even then, it was only half a quip. For Rivière liked to say that "if the insomnia of a musician causes him to create beautiful works, it is a beautiful insomnia." One day, pointing to Leroux, he had said: "Look at that! What beauty there is in the ugliness that repels love! ..." Leroux may well have owed his finest qualities to this misfortune, which had forced him to live only for his job.

"Are you a close friend of Pellerin's?"

"Er ..."

"I'm not holding it against you."

Rivière faced about and with his eyes fixed on the floor he took a few short steps, with Robineau beside him. A sad smile came to his lips for some reason Robineau could not fathom.

"Only ... only ... you are the boss."

"Yes," said Robineau.

Every night, thought Rivière, some new action, like a drama, was unfolding in the sky. Any slackening of willpower could entail defeat, and between now and dawn the struggle might be grim.

"You must keep your place." Rivière weighed his words. "Tomorrow night you may have to order this pilot out on a dangerous flight. He will have to obey."

"Yes."

"Upon you depends the life and welfare of men, and of men who are worth more than you ..." He seemed to hesitate. "That's a serious matter."

Still pacing up and down with small neat steps, Rivière let several seconds go by.

"If it's out of a feeling of friendship that they obey you, then you are deceiving them. You yourself have no right to ask a sacrifice of them."

"No, of course not."

"And if they think that your friendship will spare

34

them certain unpleasant chores, you are also deceiving them. For they have no choice but to obey. Now sit down there."

Gently Rivière pushed Robineau towards his office.

"Robineau, I'm going to teach you a lesson. If you feel tired, it's not the job of these men to buck you up. You are the boss. Your weakness is ridiculous. Now write . . ."

"I . . ."

"Write: 'Inspector Robineau imposes such and such a penalty on the pilot Pellerin for such and such a motive . . .' It's up to you to find the motive."

"Monsieur le Directeur!"

"Act as though you understood, Robineau. Love the men you command—but without telling them."

Robineau, once more, would see to it that the propeller-bosses were zealously scrubbed.

*

A radio message from an emergency landing-strip announced: "Plane in sight. Plane signals: reduced engine speed, am landing."

That would almost certainly mean a half hour lost. Rivière felt the irritation the traveller experiences when the express train comes to a halt on the track and the minutes no longer yield their crop of passing plains. The large clock-hand would now traverse an empty space, within whose ample compass so many events might have been fitted. To while away the interval Rivière left his office: the night now seemed empty like a stage without actors. "A night like this wasted!" he thought, as he stared out of the window. He was irked by this cloudless sky bejewelled with stars and that moon vainly squandering its gold among the twinkling ground-lights of heaven.

*

But once the plane had taken off, the night for Rivière was once more filled with beauty and enchantment. Its loins were now quick with life, and Rivière was its custodian.

"What kind of weather have you?" he had the radio operator ask the crew. Ten seconds passed.

"Very fine."

Then came the names of several more towns overflown, and for Rivière, in this battle, they had the sound of vanquished cities.

VII

An hour later the radio operator of the Patagonia mail-plane felt himself softly heaved up, as by a giant shoulder. He looked about him: heavy clouds were extinguishing the stars. He leaned over and peered down at the earth, looking for the lights of villages, hidden like glow-worms in the fields, but nothing shone in this black grass.

He felt depressed, foreseeing a difficult night—

with marches, countermarches, and occupied territories they would have to yield. He didn't understand the pilot's tactics; for a little farther on, it seemed to him, they would butt up against the thickness of the night as against a wall.

Directly in front of them he could now perceive a faint glimmer on the rim of the horizon, the pale glow of a forge. The radio operator tapped Fabien's shoulder, but the pilot did not budge.

The first tremors of the distant storm began hitting the plane. Gently heaving up, its metal mass compressed the radio operator's flesh, then seemed to relax and melt into the night, leaving him for several seconds floating weightlessly. Convulsively he gripped the metal spars on either side. Now that there was nothing more of the world to be seen than the red cockpit lamp, he shuddered at the thought that they were dropping into the heart of the night, helpless and with only a small miner's lamp to guide him. He dared not disturb the pilot to find out what he intended doing; and, his hands gripped around the steel, he lent tensely forward, staring at the dark form ahead of him.

A head and two unmoving shoulders were all that could be seen in the dim light. The pilot's body was a dark mass, slightly humped over to the left, his face turned towards the storm and doubtless washed by its flickering flashes. The radio operator could see nothing of this face: hidden from him were the feelings that were being mustered to deal with the storm—the tight-set lips, the determination, the anger, the elemental exchange taking place between this pale face and those brief flashes in the distance.

Yet he could sense the strength concentrated in that immobile shadow, and he liked it. It was carrying him towards the storm, but it also shielded him. Those hands, gripping the controls, weighed already on the storm as on the neck of a wild beast, but the strong shoulders remained motionless, attesting deep reserves of strength. After all, the radio operator thought to himself, the pilot was responsible. So now, borne like a pillion-rider on this gallop towards the blaze, he relished what the dark form in front of him conjured up in material weight and durability.

To the left, as faint as a flashing beacon, a new fire was kindled. The radio operator reached forward to touch Fabien's shoulder by way of warning, but he saw him slowly turn his head and stare this new enemy in the face for several seconds, then slowly revert to his original position. His shoulders were as motionless as ever, like the back of his head, solidly pressed against the leather pad.

VIII

Rivière had gone out to stretch his legs a bit and to forget the malaise which kept nagging at him. He who only lived for dramatic action now felt a curious shifting of the drama as it became more personal. Grouped about their bandstands, he reflected, the middle-class inhabitants of little towns lived lives that were outwardly sedate yet sometimes marked by crises—illness, love, bereavements—and who knows? ... his own malaise was proving similarly instructive. "It opens windows," he thought, "on many things."

Feeling refreshed, he turned and headed back towards the office. It was almost eleven. Crowds had gathered in front of the cinemas and he had to shoulder his way through them. He raised his eyes towards the stars, glittering faintly above the narrow street, almost obliterated by the bright neon signs, and thought: "Tonight, with two mail-planes in the air, I am responsible for an entire sky. That star up there is a sign, searching me out and finding me in this crowd. It's why I feel something of a stranger, a bit lonely."

A musical phrase came back to him, some notes in a sonata he had been listening to the day before with some friends. His friends had not understood it. "This music bores us and you too, only you won't admit it."

"Perhaps ..." he had answered.

Then, as again tonight, he had felt lonely, but he had quickly realized the wealth of such a solitude. The message of this music had reached him, alone among these humdrum folk, with the softness of a secret. So now this star. Above all these shoulders he was being spoken to in a tongue which he alone could hear.

Someone jostled him on the pavement. "I won't get angry," he thought. "I'm like the father of a sick child, walking with short steps in the crowd. Within him he carries the hushed silence of his house."

He looked at the people around him, seeking to recognize those among them who with little steps were out walking their invention or their love; and he thought of the loneliness of lighthouse-keepers.

*

The silence of the offices pleased him. He walked slowly through them, one after the other, his footsteps echoing hollowly. The typewriters slept beneath their covers. The big cupboard doors had closed on their shelves of well ordered files. Ten years of work and experience. He felt as though he were visiting the vaults of a bank—there where there lies a weight of gold. But each of these registers had accumulated a finer stuff than gold—a stock of living energy. Living but asleep, like hoarded gold.

Somewhere he would come upon the only clerk on night duty. The man was working somewhere so that the life of the company should know no break, so that everything might be infused with a steady determination, so that, from Toulouse to Buenos Aires, each airfield should be part of the same unbroken chain.

"That fellow," thought Rivière, "doesn't realize his greatness." Somewhere in these southern skies the mail-planes were battling their way forward. A night flight was like an illness over which one had to keep watch. One had to help these men who, with their hands and knees, chest against chest, were wrestling with the dark, who were locked in a struggle with unseen, shifting things, from whose fateful grip their blind arms had to pull them, as from a sea. What dreadful admissions he had sometimes heard! "I lit the lamp to see my hands . . ." The velvet texture of a pair of hands revealed in this dark-room glow—all that was left of the world and which must be saved.

Rivière pushed open the door of the Traffic Office. A solitary lamp in one corner made a luminous beach. The clicking of a single typewriter gave meaning to the silence, without filling it. Now and then the telephone buzzer sounded; whereupon the duty clerk got up and walked towards this sad, obstinate, repeated call. The duty clerk lifted the receiver and the invisible anguish was soothed by a soft exchange of murmurs in a shadowy corner. Then the man returned to his office, his solitude- and sleep-drawn features closed over some hermetic secret. What a latent menace there is in a call coming from the outer night when two mail-planes are in the air! Rivière thought of the telegrams which reach families under the evening lamp-light, then of the grief which for several seemingly eternal seconds remains a secret on the father's face. At first no more than a ripple, so soft, so remote from the distantly uttered cry. It was its faint echo he caught each time the telephone sounded its discreet buzzer. And each time he saw the clerk emerging from the shadows towards the lamp-light, like a diver ascending from the depths, his slow, solitary, deliberate movements struck him as heavy with secrets.

"Don't move. I'll take it."

Rivière lifted the receiver and heard the buzzing of the outer world.

"Rivière speaking."

There was a confused sound, then a voice: "I'm connecting you to the radio station."

There was a new crackling, as the operator plugged into the switchboard, then another voice came through: "This is the radio centre. Here are the latest telegrams."

Rivière took them down, nodding his head as he did so:

"Good . . . Good . . ."

Nothing of importance. The usual service messages. Rio de Janeiro asking for information, Montevideo reporting on the weather, Mendoza on a question of equipment. Familiar household noises.

"And the mail-planes?"

"There's thunder in the air. We can't hear them."

"I see."

The night was fine and starry, Rivière reflected, yet in it the radio operators could detect the breath of distant storms.

"Ring me back."

As Rivière rose, the clerk came up to him. "Some papers to be signed, sir."

"All right."

Rivière felt a mounting fondness for this man, upon whom the night also weighed. "A comrade-

in-arms," he thought. "And who may never know
how much this vigil has brought us together."

IX

As he was walking back to his office with a sheaf
of papers in his hand, Rivière felt a stab of pain in
his right side. For some weeks now it had been
bothering him.

"Bad . . ."

He leaned for a moment against the wall.

"How ridiculous!" he thought, as he made his
way to his chair.

Once again he felt himself chained up, like an
ageing lion, and a great sadness came over him.

"So much work and effort to end up like this! I'm
fifty years old. At fifty I've had a full life, I've
struggled, I've altered the course of events, yet here
I am tormented by something that makes everything
else seem trifling . . . Ridiculous!"

He paused, wiped away several drops of sweat,
and when the pain had eased, he set to work on the
memoranda.

"In taking down Motor 301 in Buenos Aires we
discovered that . . . The person responsible will be
severely fined."

He signed.

"The Florianopolis airfield, having failed to heed
instructions . . ."

He signed.

"As a disciplinary measure we are transferring airfield controller Richard for having . . ."

He signed.

Slumbering but ever present in him, like a new meaning of life, the pain in his side brought his thoughts back on himself.

"Am I being fair or not?" he wondered, almost bitterly. "I don't know. If I bear down hard, the accidents diminish. It isn't the individual who's responsible; it's an obscure power that can only be dealt with if everyone is affected. If I were really fair and just, each night flight would involve a risk of death."

He felt a certain weariness at having traced so hard a road. Pity, he thought, is good. He leafed through the papers, absorbed in his reflections.

" . . . As for Roblet, as of today he is no longer part of our personnel."

He recalled the talk he had had with the old fellow the evening before.

"An example, you understand, is an example."

"But Monsieur . . . but Monsieur . . . It was only once, one single time, just think! I who've worked all my life!"

"An example must be made."

"But Monsieur! . . . Look, Monsieur!"

He had produced a tattered pocket-book and pulled from it a yellowed newspaper page which showed Roblet posing in front of a plane. Rivière had seen the old hands trembling over this naive glory.

"This dates from 1910, Monsieur ... It was me here assembled the first plane in Argentina! I've been in aviation since 1910, Monsieur ... Twenty years, that makes! So how can you say ... And the young 'uns, Monsieur, how they'll be laughing in the workshops! ... Oh, but how they'll laugh!"

"I can't help that."

"And my kids, Monsieur, my kids!"

"I told you—you can stay on as an odd job man."

"But my dignity, Monsieur, my dignity! Just think, Monsieur, twenty years of aviation, an old worker like me ..."

"As an odd job man, I said."

"I refuse, Monsieur, I refuse!"

The old hands had trembled, and Rivière had had to avert his eyes from that thick, wrinkled, lovely skin.

"As an odd job man ..."

"No, Monsieur, no ... And there's something else I want to say—"

"That will do."

"It wasn't him I was so brutally dismissing," thought Rivière, "it was the trouble for which he's perhaps not responsible but of which he's the agent. Men are paltry things, and they too must be created. Or eliminated when they bring bad luck."

"And there's something else I want to say ..." What had the poor fellow meant by that? That he was being deprived of his old joys? That he enjoyed the sound of his tools against the steel of the planes, that his life would be robbed of its poetry ... and then, a man must live?

"I'm tired," thought Rivière, feeling faintly feverish. He drummed his finger on the sheet of paper. "I liked that old worker's face ..." Rivière thought of his hands, of the tiny movement that could have brought them together. He had only needed to say: "All right. All right. You can stay." Rivière imagined the joy which would have gushed through those old hands. And the joy which those old workman's hands, even more than his face, would have expressed struck him as the loveliest thing in all the world. "Shall I tear up this memorandum?"

And what a homecoming in the evening, what a modest pride in the presence of the family!

"So they're keeping you on?"

"What do you think! It was me assembled the first plane in Argentina!"

And the young ones who would no longer laugh at the old timer's lost prestige ...

"Shall I tear it up?"

The telephone rang. Rivière lifted the receiver. There was a long pause, then that resonance, that depth which the wind and space lend to human voices. Finally a voice spoke:

"Airfield here. Who's that?"

"Rivière."

"Monsieur le Directeur, the 650 is on the field and ready."

"Good."

"Well, everything's now under control. But at the

last moment we had to redo the electric circuit, there were some faulty connections."

"I see. Who did the wiring?"

"We'll check. And with your permission we'll take the necessary disciplinary action. A light failure on the instrument panel can be a serious matter."

"Of course."

"If," Rivière thought, "one doesn't uproot the trouble wherever one meets it, light failures will occur. It would have been criminal to have found it out only when the pilot had to light up his instruments. Roblet shall go."

The clerk, who had seen nothing, was still typing away.

"What's that?"

"The fortnightly accounts."

"Why aren't they ready?"

"I . . ."

"I'll look into it."

Strange, how easily events get the upper hand! Rivière thought of those clinging vines that are strong enough to bring down temples. It was the same elemental force at work in the rain forests, the same upheaving force which threatens any great undertaking.

"A great undertaking . . ."

To reassure himself he added: "I like all of these men. It's not them I'm fighting, it's the ill that passes through them."

He could feel his heart beat faster and it hurt him.

"I don't know if what I've done is good. I don't

know the exact value of human life, nor of justice, nor of grief. I don't know exactly what a man's joy is worth. Nor a trembling hand. Nor pity, nor kindness . . .

"Life is so full of contradictions," he reflected. "One manages as best one can . . . But creating, making things last, exchanging one's perishable body . . . ?"

Rivière, after a moment of reflection, rang his bell.

"Telephone the pilot of the Europe-bound plane and tell him to come and see me before taking off.

"There's no point," he thought, "in the mail-plane's pointlessly turning back. If I don't shake my men up, the night will always unnerve them."

X

Woken by the telephone, the pilot's wife looked at her husband and thought: "I'll let him sleep a little longer."

She gazed admiringly at his naked chest, beautifully rounded like a ship's hull. He lay in this calm bed, as in a harbour, and lest anything disturb his slumbers, she smoothed out this fold, this shadow, this wave, with her finger, stilling this bed as a divine finger does the sea.

She got up and opened the window. The wind hit her in the face. Their bedroom overlooked Buenos Aires. People were dancing in a nearby house, the wind brought the sound of music, for it was the hour of pleasure and repose. The city had packed its inhabitants into a hundred thousand fortresses: everything was peaceful and secure; but it seemed to this woman that a cry would soon ring out: "To arms!" and that only one man, her own, would rise up in answer. He was still resting, but his rest was the redoubtable, fragile repose of reserves soon to be committed. This sleeping city offered him no protection: vain would soon seem its lights when, like a young god, he soared above their glittering dust. She looked at those stout arms which in an hour's time would shoulder the burden of the Europe-bound mail and be responsible for something big, like the fate of a city. The thought troubled her. That this man, among millions of others, was alone prepared for this strange sacrifice made her sad. He would soon be beyond the range of her tenderness. She had fed him, watched over him, caressed him not for herself but for this night which was going to claim him. For struggles, anxieties, and victories she would never know anything about. Those tender hands of his had merely been tamed, and the real work for which they were destined remained obscure. She knew this man's smiles, his thoughtfulness as a lover, but not his godlike fury in a storm. She burdened him with tender links—music, love, flowers—but at the moment of each take-off these links were cast off without his seeming to feel regret.

He opened his eyes.

"What's the time?"

"Midnight."

"How's the weather?"

"I don't know."

He got up, and stretching lazily, walked towards the window.

"I shouldn't be too cold. Which way is the wind blowing?"

"How should I know?"

He leaned out. "From the south. That's fine. It should hold as far as Brazil."

He looked up at the moon and felt like a millionaire. Then he looked down on the city, finding it neither kind nor luminous nor warm. He could already see its lights . . . draining out their vain sands.

"What are you thinking of?"

He was thinking of the fog he might run into in the region of Porto Allegre.

"I've worked out my tactics. I know exactly how to get around it."

He was still bent over the window-sill, inhaling deeply, as though about to dive naked into the sea.

"You're not even sad . . . How many days will you be gone?"

Eight, ten days, he didn't know. Sad, no . . . why? Those plains, those towns, those mountains . . . He was setting forth like a free man on their conquest. In an hour's time Buenos Aires would have been vanquished and then discarded behind him.

He smiled: "This city . . . I'll soon be far from it. It's a lovely thing, leaving at night. You pull the throttle lever all the way back, headed south, and ten seconds later you swing the landscape round and head north. The city disappears, like an ocean bottom."

She thought of all the things a man must reject in order to conquer.

"Don't you like your home?"

"I do like my home."

But his wife knew that he was already on his way. His broad shoulders were already bearing into the sky.

She pointed to it. "You've got lovely weather, your route is paved with stars."

"Yes," he laughed.

She laid her hand on his shoulder: it seemed almost unnaturally warm, as though the flesh were threatened by some inner ferment.

"You're very strong, I know, but do be careful!"

"Careful? Of course . . ." And he laughed again.

He began dressing. For this fiesta he chose the roughest materials, the heaviest of leather gear, he dressed like a peasant. The heavier he grew, the more she admired him. She buckled his belt herself, helped him pull on his boots.

"These boots are too tight."

"Here are the others."

"Fetch me a piece of cord for the emergency lamp."

She looked at him. She was helping to repair the last chinks in the armour. Now everything was set.

"You look wonderful."

She watched him, carefully combing his hair.

"Is it for the stars?"

"So I won't start feeling old . . ."

"I'm jealous . . ."

He laughed again and kissed her, pressing her against his heavy togs. Then he lifted her up on outstretched arms, much as one lifts a little girl, and still laughing, he laid her out on the bed.

"Now go to sleep!"

Closing the door behind him, he descended into the street. Here, in the midst of the anonymous night crowd, he took his first conquering steps.

She remained behind, gazing sadly at the flowers, the books, the tender souvenirs—for him a mere ocean bottom.

XI

Rivière greeted him: "That was a neat one you pulled on me during your last flight. Turning back when the weather reports were good. You could have pushed through. You were scared?"

Taken aback, the pilot said nothing. He rubbed his hands slowly against each other. Then he raised his head and looked Rivière in the eyes.

"Yes."

Rivière felt sorry for this brave fellow who had taken fright. The pilot sought to apologize:

"I couldn't see a blessed thing. I know . . . further on perhaps . . . The radio said so . . . But my panel lamp got so dim I couldn't even see my hands.

I tried switching on my wing-light, but I couldn't see that either. It was like being at the bottom of a deep hole it's hard to climb out of. And then, my engine began vibrating . . ."

"No."

"No?"

"No. We had a look at it afterwards. It was in perfect shape. But one always thinks an engine's vibrating when one's scared."

"Who wouldn't have been scared! There were mountains all round and above me. When I tried climbing, I ran into a lot of turbulence. You know—when one's as blind as a bat—the downdraughts . . . Instead of climbing, I lost three hundred feet. I couldn't see the artificial horizon, I couldn't even see the oil-pressure gauge any more. I had the impression my engine was losing speed, that it was heating up and the oil pressure going down . . . And all of it in the dark, like a tomb. I was damned glad to see the lights of the first town again."

"You've got too much imagination. Now be off with you."

And the pilot left him.

*

Rivière sank back in his chair and ran his fingers through his grey hair.

"He's the bravest of my men," he thought. "That was a fine piece of piloting the other night, but even so . . . I rescue him from fear."

For a moment he yielded to a new wave of indulgence. "To make oneself loved, it's enough to show pity. I show scant pity, or I hide it. Yet I wouldn't mind surrounding myself with friendship and human kindness. A doctor encounters them in his profession. But I'm the servant of events. I must forge men so that they can serve them too. How harshly I feel this iron law, here in my office in the evening when I'm alone with the flight reports. But if I let myself go, if I let events take their well ordered course, then accidents mysteriously occur. As though it were my sole will which kept the plane from cracking up in flight, or the storm from slowing down the mail. Sometimes I'm surprised by my own power."

"Probably it's quite straightforward," he mused on. "Like the gardener's never-ending struggle with his lawn. It's the simple weight of his hand, bearing down ceaselessly upon it, which keeps the earth from throwing up a jungle."

He thought of the pilot. "I'm rescuing him from fear. It's not him I was attacking, but through him that resistance which paralyses men in the face of the unknown. If I listen to him, if I feel sorry for him, if I take his apprehensions seriously, he will think he's returning from a land of mystery, and mystery alone is what one is afraid of. There must be no more mystery. The men must descend into this dark well, and then come up again saying they've found nothing. This man must descend into the innermost heart of the night, in all its depth, and without so much as that little miner's lamp which, though it only lights up the hands or the wing, keeps the unknown at arm's length."

*

Yet in this battle a silent fraternity bound Rivière to his pilots. They were crew-mates, fired with the same desire to vanquish. But Rivière recalled the other battles he had had to wage for the conquest of the night. In official circles this dark territory was feared like an unexplored hinterland. The idea of launching a crew at 140 miles an hour against the thunderstorms and mists and all the material obstacles that night secretes, seemed to them an adventure which was tolerable for military aviation: when the night is clear one takes off, drops bombs, and returns to the same field. But regular mail flights were bound to fail. "For us," Rivière had replied, "it's a matter of life and death, since we lose at night the lead we gain each day on the railways and steamships."

Rivière had been forced to listen to much boring talk about balance-sheets, insurance rates, and, above all, public opinion. "Public opinion," he retorted, "is something one guides, one governs." What a waste of time! he had thought. "There's something ... something infinitely more important than all this. A thing which is really alive upsets everything, it generates its own laws for living. It's irresistible." Rivière had no idea when or how commercial aviation would undertake night flights, but one had to prepare for this unavoidable solution.

He recalled those green baize table covers in front of which, his chin resting on his fist, he had had to listen to so many objections. How vain they had seemed to him, how condemned in advance by life! And with them he had felt his own strength gathering weight within him. "My reasons carry weight, I'll win," Rivière had thought. "It's the natural slope of events." When they asked him for perfect solutions, guaranteed to eliminate all risks, he would reply: "Experience will establish the necessary laws. The proper understanding of laws never precedes experience."

Rivière had finally won, after a long year of battling. For some it was "because of his faith", for others "because of his bear-like tenacity and toughness". But for him it was simply because he was leaning in the right direction.

But how cautious the first steps had been! The planes only took off one hour before sunrise and landed one hour after sunset. Only when Rivière felt surer of his ground did he dare push his mail-planes into the depths of the night. Backed up by almost nobody, disowned by nearly all, he now waged a lonely battle.

Rivière rang, to get the latest messages from the planes in flight.

XII

The Patagonia mail-plane was now entering the storm. Fabien gave up all thought of trying to fly around it: its front was too broad, and the battle-line of lightning flashes extended far inland, revealing mighty fortresses of cloud. He would try to slip through underneath, and if the going got too rough, he would turn and fly out.

He glanced at his altimeter: 1,700 metres. He pressed the palms of his hands against the controls to lose height. The engine throbbed wildly and the plane began to tremble. Fabien corrected the angle of descent, then looked at the map to check the height of the hills beneath him. 500 metres. To keep a safe margin he would fly at 700. He was sacrificing his altitude as one stakes a fortune.

The plane lurched, trembling, into an air pocket. Fabien felt himself threatened by invisible landslides. He thought wistfully of turning back to find his hundred thousand stars, but he did not shift his course by one degree.

Fabien calculated his chances. Probably this was a local storm; for Trelew, the next port-of-call, reported a sky that was only three-quarters overcast. He had just twenty more minutes of this inky concrete to endure. Yet the pilot felt uneasy. Hunched over to the left, into the teeth of the wind, he sought to interpret those confused glows which permeate even the most opaque of nights. But there was now not even a glow: only changes of density in the surrounding darkness, or was it a fatigue of the eyes?

He unfolded a slip of paper handed to him by the radio operator: "Where are we?"

Fabien would have given a great deal to know. He scribbled back: "Don't know. We're crossing storm by compass."

He hunched over once again. He was bothered by the exhaust flame ahead of him, pinned to the engine like a bouquet of fire, so pale that the moonlight would have extinguished it, but which in this inky void absorbed the visible world. He watched it—braided stiffly by the wind, like a torch flame.

Every thirty seconds, to check his gyroscope and compass readings, Fabien ducked his head down inside the cockpit. He no longer dared light the dim red panel-lamps which would have blinded him for too long an interval, but the dials with their radium-tinted numbers emitted a pale star-like glow. Here, amid dial-hands and figures, the pilot experienced a deceptive security, such as one feels in a ship's cabin overswept by waves. The night, and all it secreted of rocks and reefs and wreckage, came billowing up against the plane with the same startling fatality.

"Where are we?" again queried the radio operator.

Fabien had straightened up and resumed his grim watch, bent over to the left for a better view beyond the motor. He had no idea how much time or effort it would take to deliver himself from these dark thongs, or if he would ever be freed of them. He was gambling his life on the brief message scrawled on this dirty, crumpled slip of paper he had unfolded and re-read a thousand times, to sustain his hopes: "Trelew: sky three-quarters overcast, weak west wind." If Trelew was three-quarters overcast, its lights could soon be spotted through a rift in the clouds. Unless . . .

The pale glow promised him up ahead prompted him to carry on. But to still his doubts he scribbled back to the radio operator: "Don't know if I can get through. Find out if weather's still fine behind."

The reply appalled him:

"Comodoro reports: return here impossible. Storm."

He was beginning to take the measure of this unusual offensive, launched from the cordillera of the Andes towards the sea. Before he could reach them, the cyclone would have scooped up all the towns.

"Ask state of weather at San Antonio."

"Reply from San Antonio: rising west wind, storm to west. Sky four-quarters overcast. San Antonio receiving very badly because of static. I'm hearing badly too. May have to haul in aerial soon because of lightning discharges. Are you turning back? What are your plans?"

"Stuff your questions. Ask for weather at Bahía Blanca."

"Reply from Bahía Blanca: violent west gale expected over Bahía Blanca in next twenty minutes."

"Ask for weather at Trelew."

"Reply from Trelew: west wind gale force thirty metres per second and rain squalls."

"Radio to Buenos Aires: blocked on all sides, storm developing thousand kilometre front, visibility nil. What should we do?"

*

This night for the pilot was without a landfall. It led to no port (for they all seemed inaccessible), still less towards the sun. In an hour and forty minutes the fuel supply would be exhausted. Sooner or later they would be forced to founder blindly in this sea of pitch.

If only he could make it through to dawn! Fabien thought of the dawn as of a golden strand on to which they would have been cast up after this rough night. Beneath the threatened craft the plains would spread their crib. The tranquil earth would heave into view, carrying its sleeping farms and the flocks upon its hills. Night dispelled, the storm-tossed derelicts would no longer threaten rack and ruin. If he could have done so, how he would have swum towards the daylight!

But now he was encircled. Everything, for good or ill, would be resolved in this thick murk. Yes, it was true: the onset of day was like a convalescence. He had felt it more than once, but never more poignantly than now. What good was it to train one's eyes on the east, the sun's distant home? Between them now there lay such an abyss of night that from its depths never could he rise.

XIII

"The Asunción mail-plane is doing well. It should get in around two o'clock. On the other hand, the Patagonia mail-plane seems to be in trouble and we can anticipate a serious delay."

"Yes, Monsieur Rivière."

"We may possibly not wait for its arrival before having the Europe plane take off. As soon as Asunción is in, you'll ring me for instructions. Meanwhile stand by."

Rivière now scanned the weather reports from the airfields to the north. They promised the Europe-bound mail-plane a perfect moonlit ride. "Sky clear, full moon, no wind." The mountains of Brazil, darkly silhouetted against the moon-flooded heavens, plunged their shocks of jet-black forest into the silvery undulations of the sea. Those forests upon which, without colouring them, the moonbeams unwearyingly rained down. Black too were the islands, floating on the sea like derelicts. And above them all the moon, that fount of light!

If Rivière ordered the take-off, the crew of the Europe-bound mail-plane would enter a stable world, softly glowing all night long. A world in which nothing threatened the equilibrium of shadowed masses and wells of light. A world unruffled by the faintest caress of those pure winds which, though they cool, can spoil an entire sky in a couple of hours.

Yet Rivière hesitated before this beckoning radiance, like a prospector in front of forbidden goldfields. The situation in the south threatened to prove him wrong. From a disaster in Patagonia his adversaries could derive such moral backing that it might well reduce his faith to impotence. Rivière was the sole champion of night flights, but his faith remained unshaken. A flaw in his work had made the crisis possible: the crisis had shown up the flaw, it proved nothing more. "We may need observation posts in the west. It's something we'll look into," he thought. "I'll have the same solid reasons for insisting. It will be one less possible cause of accident, the one that's now shown up."

Strong men are fortified by setbacks. Unfortunately, in dealing with men one plays a game in which the real meaning of things counts for little. People win or lose on the basis of appearances, and the points gained are trivial. A semblance of defeat is enough to hamstring one completely.

Rivière rang his bell.

"Still no messages from Bahía Blanca?"

"No."

"Get me the airfield by telephone."

Five minutes later he was through.

"Why haven't you been radioing anything?"

"We can't hear the mail-plane."

"Is he silent?"

"We don't know. There's too much thunder. Even if he was tapping something out, we'd hear nothing."

"Can Trelew hear him?"

"We can't hear Trelew."

"Then telephone."

"We've tried, but the line's cut."

"What's your weather like?"

"Pretty threatening. Lightning to west and south. Very sultry."

"Any wind?"

"Still weak, but probably not for more than ten minutes. The lightning flashes are moving up fast."

There was a pause.

"Bahía Blanca? Are you listening? Good. Call back in ten minutes."

Rivière leafed through the telegrams from the southern airfields. All alike reported: no message from the plane. Some stations no longer answered Buenos Aires. The patch of silence was spreading across the map, as the little towns were swallowed up by the cyclone, their bolted doors and lightless streets as cut off from the world and lost in the night as a ship. Dawn alone would deliver them.

Bent over the map, Rivière still hoped against hope to discover a tiny haven of clear sky. He had dispatched telegrams to thirty provincial police-stations requesting information on the weather. The

63

replies were beginning to come in. Over a distance of twelve hundred miles the radio stations were instructed to notify Buenos Aires within thirty seconds if one of them intercepted an appeal from the plane, so that the position of the haven could be relayed back to Fabien.

The secretaries, reporting for night duty at 1 a.m., were now in their offices. Hurried whispers made it known that night flights would probably be suspended, and that the Europe-bound mail would not take off before dawn. They spoke in hushed tones of Fabien, the cyclone, and above all of Rivière, whom they could picture nearby, crushed by the growing magnitude of this elemental rebuff.

Abruptly the chattering stopped. Rivière had just appeared, pausing by his door in his overcoat, the hat still pulled down over the eyes, like the eternal voyager he seemed to be. He stepped quietly up to the head clerk.

"It's 1.10. Are the clearance papers for the Europe mail in order?"

"I . . . I thought—"

"You're not here to think, but to carry out orders."

He turned slowly on his heel and walked over to an open window, his hands clasped behind his back.

A secretary caught up with him: "Monsieur le Directeur, we won't be getting many replies. We've been informed that inland many telephone lines are already down."

"I see."

Without moving a muscle Rivière stared out at the night.

*

Thus each new message boded new peril for the mail. Each town able to reply before the telephone lines were wrecked reported the advance of the cyclone, like that of an invasion. "It's coming from the interior, from the cordillera. It's sweeping everything before it towards the sea . . ."

Rivière looked up at the stars. They were too bright and the air was too humid. What a strange night! It was rotting away in patches, like the flesh of a glowing peach. The stars in all their glory still shone down on Buenos Aires, but they were no more than an oasis, and a temporary one at that. A haven which in any case was beyond Fabien's reach. A night of menace, touched and tainted by an evil wind. A difficult night to overcome.

Somewhere in its depths a plane was in peril; but here on the bank one waved one's arms in vain.

XIV

Fabien's wife telephoned.

Each time he was due back she would calculate the progress of the Patagonia mail-plane. "He's now taking off from Trelew . . ." And she would go back to sleep. A little later: "He must be approaching

San Antonio, he should be able to see its lights . . ."
She would then get up, throw back the curtains, and
question the sky. "Those clouds will bother him . . ."
At times the moon was there, ready to shepherd him
across the heavens. Whereupon the young wife went
back to bed, reassured by the moon and the stars, by
those thousand and one presences hovering over her
husband. Towards one o'clock she would feel him
drawing near. "He can't be far off now, he must be
in sight of Buenos Aires . . ." She then got up once
more and prepared a meal for him, with a pot of hot
coffee. "It's so cold up there . . ." She always wel-
comed him back as though he had just descended
from some snowy summit. "Aren't you cold?"
"Why no." "Well, warm yourself anyway . . ."
At 1.15, when everything was ready, she would
telephone.

Tonight, as on the others, she rang up to get the
news.

"Has Fabien landed?"

The secretary at the other end began to fumble
for his words.

"Who's speaking?"

"Simone Fabien."

"Ah! Just a moment . . ."

Not daring to say anything, the secretary passed
the receiver to the head clerk.

"Who is it?"

"Simone Fabien."

"Ah! . . . What can I do for you, Madame?"

"Has my husband landed?"

There was a baffling silence, followed by this simple reply: "No."

"Has he been held up?"

"Yes."

There was another silence. "Yes, he's been held up."

"Ah!"

That "Ah!" was the cry of a wounded creature. Being held up is nothing . . . is nothing . . . but when it lasts too long . . .

"Ah! . . . And when is he expected in?"

"When's he expected in? We . . . we don't know exactly."

It was like talking to a wall. All she was getting now was echoes of her own questions.

"Do please tell me, give me an answer! Where is he?"

"Where is he? Wait . . ."

The suspense was painful. Something was going on there, behind that wall.

An answer was finally forthcoming.

"He took off from Comodoro at 19.30."

"And since then?"

"Since then? . . . He's been seriously delayed . . . seriously delayed by bad weather . . ."

"Ah! Bad weather!"

What injustice, what sly deceit on the part of that lazy moon, languidly stretched out up there over Buenos Aires! Suddenly the young wife remembered that barely two hours were needed to fly from Comodoro to Trelew.

"And he's been flying six hours towards Trelew! But he's been sending out messages! What's he been saying?"

"What's he been saying? Naturally ... with this kind of weather ... you understand ... his messages haven't been getting through ..."

"This kind of weather!"

"Madame, rest assured. We'll call you the moment we know something."

"Oh! So you know nothing!"

"Good-bye, Madame ..."

"No! No! I want to talk to the Director."

"Monsieur le Directeur is very busy, Madame, he's got someone in his office ..."

"Well, I don't care! I don't care! I want to talk to him!"

The head clerk mopped his brow. "Just a moment, please ..."

He pushed open Rivière's door.

"It's Madame Fabien ... wants to speak to you ..."

"What I was dreading!" thought Rivière. The emotional facets of the crisis were beginning to manifest themselves. His first impulse was to brush them aside: mothers and wives are not admitted to Operations Rooms. Emotional outbursts are likewise silenced on a ship in danger. They are no help in saving lives. Nevertheless he agreed to take the call.

"Switch it through to my office."

He heard that distant, trembling voice and instantly realized that he could give her no answer.

It would be pointless, utterly futile for them to meet face to face.

"Madame, I beg you, please calm yourself! In our profession we often have to wait a long time for news."

He had reached that frontier where the issue was not a tiny individual distress, but the problem posed by action. Facing Rivière now was not Fabien's wife, but another form of life. Rivière could only listen, could only pity that small voice, that desperate plaint, but it was that of the enemy. For action and individual happiness know no quarter: they are in conflict. This woman also was speaking in the name of a world of absolute rights and duties—that of the lamp-light on the evening table, of a flesh which claims its flesh, of a homeland of hopes, affections, and remembrances. She claimed her own and she was right. Rivière too was right; but he could oppose nothing to this woman's truth. His own truth was revealed to him in the light of a humble domestic lamp—inexpressible, inhuman . . .

"Madame . . ."

She was no longer listening. She had slumped down, it seemed to him, at his feet, her feeble fists exhausted from beating on the wall.

*

An engineer had one day said to Rivière, as they were bending over an injured man, near a bridge that was being built: "Is this bridge worth the price of a

69

crushed face?" Not one of the peasants for whom this road was being opened would have agreed in advance to the mutilation of this face, simply to spare himself a detour via the next bridge. Yet one went on building bridges. The engineer had added: "The general interest is made up of individual interests: it does not justify anything else."

"And yet," Rivière had replied to him later, "if human life is priceless, we always act as though there was something exceeding human life in value . . . But what?"

Now, thinking of the airborne crew, Rivière felt a pang. Action, even that involved in the building of a bridge, breaks hearts, and Rivière could no longer avoid asking himself "in the name of what?"

"These men," he thought, "who are perhaps doomed to disappear, could have lived happily." He imagined their faces crowded around the golden sanctuary of evening lamps. "In the name of what did I tear them from it?" In the name of what had he torn them from individual happiness? Was not one's first obligation to protect this kind of happiness? Yet he himself was shattering it. Still, the golden sanctuaries one day vanish inexorably like mirages. Old age and death destroy them, even more pitilessly than he. Perhaps there is something else, something more enduring to be saved; and perhaps it was to save this part of man that Rivière was working? Otherwise, the action would have no justification.

*

"To love, only to love, what an impasse!" Rivière had the obscure sentiment of a duty greater than that of loving. Or perhaps it was also a form of affection, but so different from the rest. A phrase came back to him: "It's a question of making them eternal . . ." Where had he read that? "That which you seek within yourself will die." He recalled a temple erected by the ancient Incas of Peru in honour of the Sun-God, those sharp-cut stones against the mountainside. But for them what would there be left of a powerful civilization which now weighed, with all the weight of its massive stones, like a reproach on contemporary man? "In the name of what harshness, of what strange love did the leader of men of yore force the multitudes to drag this temple up the mountain, thus compelling them to erect their own eternity?" And there arose in Rivière's mind the vision of the crowds in little provincial towns, strolling around their bandstands in the evening. "This kind of happiness, this harness . . ." he thought. But the leader of men of yore, if he felt scant pity for man's sufferings, felt a boundless pity for his death. Not for his individual death, but pity for the species, doomed one day to be erased like footprints in the sand. And he drove his people to erect stones which the desert would not bury.

XV

This slip of neatly folded paper might perhaps save him: Fabien unfolded it, his jaw grimly
set.

"Can't get through to Buenos Aires. Can't even
tap out a message, getting electric shocks in my
fingers."

Irritated, Fabien wanted to reply, but the moment
he took his hands off the controls to write, he felt
his body heaved up by a mighty groundswell. The
air currents lifted him up, along with his five tons
of metal, and tossed him about. He abandoned the
attempt. His hands closed back on the wave and
steadied its wild surge.

Fabien took a deep breath. If the radio operator
hauled up the aerial because he was afraid of the
lightning, he would punch his face in when they
landed. They absolutely had to get in touch with
Buenos Aires—as though from a distance of a
thousand miles a life-line could be thrown to them in
this abyss. In the absence of a trembling light, of an
inn-lamp's distant glimmer—useless, to be sure, but
which, like a beacon, would have proved the proxim-
ity of solid land—he needed a voice, just one, come
from a world which had ceased to exist. The pilot
raised and shook his fist in the reddish glow, to make
the man behind understand this tragic truth, but the
latter failed to see it, fixed as his eyes were on the

wasteland below, with its dead lights and buried towns.

Fabien would have heeded any advice if only it could have been shouted through to him. "If they tell me to fly round in circles, I'll fly round in circles, and if they tell me to fly due south . . ." Somewhere they still existed, those lands of calm, moon-shadowed peace. Down there, like learned scientists, his omniscient companions were bent over their maps, sheltered by lamps as soft as flowers. But all it was given him to know was the turbulence of this black night, which kept pounding him with land-slides and cataracts. How could they abandon these two men amid these downpours and flame-filled clouds? How could they? "Set course at 240 de-grees . . ." they would order Fabien, and he would shift his course to 240. But he was alone.

Even the brute matter, it now seemed to him, began to mutiny. With each new plunge the engine began vibrating so violently that the entire plane was seized with angry trembling. Fabien needed all his strength to control it. His head ducked far down inside the cockpit, he kept his eyes glued to the artificial horizon; for outside he could no longer distinguish earth from sky, lost in a welter of primaeval darkness. But now the instrument needles in front of him began oscillating wildly, growing increasingly difficult to follow. Misled by their erratic readings, he lost altitude. Slowly but surely he was sinking into a dark morass, a murky quick-sand. The reading on his altimeter was now "500

73

metres"—the height of the hilltops beneath him. He could feel them heaving up their towering breakers towards him. It was as though all these land masses, the tiniest of which could have smashed him to smithereens, had suddenly been ripped from their foundations and unhinged and were now beginning to career drunkenly around him. A deadly dance had begun, tightening about him like a noose.

He made up his mind. He would land no matter where, even at the risk of cracking up. But to avoid the hills, at least, he threw out his one and only flare. It burst briefly into flame, as it spun downward, cast its eerie glow over a plain, then died: it was the sea.

The thoughts raced through his mind. "I'm lost. Even with a 40 degree wind correction, I've drifted off course. It's a gale. Where's the land?"

He banked, heading now due west. "Without a flare to guide me I'm a goner," he thought. "Well, it was bound to happen one day." As for the fellow behind him . . . "He's certain to have pulled in the aerial." But he was no longer angry with him. He had only to let go with both hands and their lives would be scattered like dust. In his hands he held the beating heart of his companion and his own. Now suddenly his hands appalled him.

At each new hammer-blow he had gripped the stick with redoubled strength, to temper the jerks which otherwise would have snapped the cables. He still hung on grimly. But now he could no longer feel his hands, numbed by the effort. He tried to move his fingers, to receive some impulse from them, but he could not tell if he was being obeyed. His arms ended in strange, almost foreign appendages—flabby and unfeeling flaps. "I must concentrate on thinking—I'm gripping." He could not tell if his thought reached his hands; for it was through the pain in his shoulders that he felt the buffets to the stick. "It's going to get away from me," he thought. "My hands are going to open ..." The mere idea that he could entertain such a thought frightened him; for he now had the impression that his hands were slowly opening in the dark and releasing their vital grip in response to the sombre image of his imagination.

He might have kept up the struggle for some time and tried his luck. There is no such thing as external fate; its real working is internal. There comes a moment when one realizes how vulnerable one is, and then the blunders suck you down, like a whirlpool.

At this very moment the storm opened above his head and through a rift, like mortal bait glittering through the meshes of a net, he spied several stars. He sensed it was a trap: one sees three stars in a hole, one rises towards them, and then one can no longer come down, one stays up there to nibble at the stars ...

But such was his thirst for light that he began to climb.

XVI

As he climbed, he found it easier to counteract the air currents by taking his bearings on the stars. Their pale magnets attracted him. He had struggled so long for a glimpse of light that now he would not have let even the faintest get away from him. Having found the inn-lamp he yearned for, he would have circled round this coveted sign till death. And thus he rose towards these fields of light.

Little by little he spiralled up in the well that had opened and which closed again beneath him. As he rose the clouds lost their muddy shadows, they swept against him in ever purer, ever whiter waves. Fabien rose clear.

His surprise was extreme. The brightness was such that it dazzled him, and for several seconds he had to close his eyes. He never would have thought that the clouds at night could dazzle. But the full moon and the constellations had changed them into radiant billows.

At a single bound, as it emerged, the plane had attained a calm that seemed wondrous. There was not a wave to rock him, and like a sail-boat passing the jetty he was entering sheltered waters. He had found refuge in some uncharted spot of sky, as hidden as the bay of the Happy Isles. Beneath him, nine thousand feet deep, the storm formed another world, shot through with gusts and cloudbursts and lightning flashes, but towards the stars it turned a surface of snowy crystal.

Fabien felt as though he had reached some strange limbo, for everything now grew luminous—his hands, his flying togs, his wings. For the light did not stream down from the stars: rather it welled up from underneath and around him from these endless white drifts. The clouds beneath him reflected back the snow shed on them by the moon, as did those banked up to right and left of him like towers. The two of them were floating through a milky stream of light. Fabien, when he looked round, saw the radio operator smiling.

"We're doing better!" he cried.

But the sound was lost in the roar of the flight, and the smiles alone came through. "I must be mad to smile," thought Fabien. "We're lost!"

A thousand dark arms had relinquished their grip on him. His bonds had been loosened, like those of a prisoner allowed to walk for a while alone among the flowers.

"Too beautiful," thought Fabien. He was wandering through a dense treasure-hoard of stars, in a world where nothing, absolutely nothing else but he, Fabien, and his companion, were alive. Similar to those thieves of fabled cities, immured within the treasure-chambers from which there is no escape. Amid the frozen gems they wander, infinitely rich yet doomed.

XVII

One of the radio operators at the Comodoro Rivadavia airfield in Patagonia made a sudden gesture, and all those who had been keeping a helpless vigil with him at the base crowded hastily around. A strong light fell on the blank sheet of paper over which they craned their necks. The radio operator's hand paused in mid-air, faintly swivelling the pencil. The radio operator's hand still held the letters captive, but already the fingers twitched.

"Thunderstorms?"

The operator nodded. The static made it difficult for him to understand. Then he scrawled a few illegible letters, then words. At last they could make out the text:

"Blocked at 12,000 feet above storm. Flying due west towards interior, having drifted out to sea. No visibility below. Can't tell if still overflying the sea. Please inform if storm extends into interior."

Because of the thunderstorms this telegram had to be relayed from base to base all the way to Buenos Aires. The message progressed through the night like a beacon, lit from watchtower to watchtower.

The reply came back from Buenos Aires: "Storm over all interior. How much fuel have you left?"

"Half an hour."

The words, relayed from post to post, travelled back to Buenos Aires.

In less than thirty minutes the plane was condemned to plunge into a cyclone that would drive it to its doom against a hidden reef of land.

XVIII

Rivière was sunk in thought. He had given up all hope: this plane would founder somewhere in the night. He recalled a scene which had greatly impressed him as a child: a pond being emptied to find a body. Here too nothing would be found until this flood of darkness had been sloughed off the earth and the sands, the plains, the wheatfields had been brought back to the light. Some humble peasants might chance upon two young bodies, their elbows crooked across their faces as though asleep, scattered through the depths of the golden grass. But the night would have drowned them.

Rivière thought of the treasures buried in the depths of the night as in fabled seas ... Night's apple-trees waiting for daybreak with their as yet unfallen blossoms. The night is rich, filled with scents and sleeping lambs and still uncoloured flowers. But bit by bit the lush furrows, the moist woods, the fresh pastures will rise towards the daylight. Among the now harmless hills and prairies, and among the little lambs two children will seem to sleep, cradled in the bosom of the world. But something will have sunk from the visible world towards the other.

Rivière was familiar with the anxious tenderness of Fabien's wife, this love that had been lent her like a toy to a poor child. And Rivière thought of Fabien's hand which for a few more minutes would hold his fate in its control. This hand that had caressed, this hand that had settled on a breast and aroused a tumult in it, like a god's. This hand that had lingered on a face and changed that face. This hand which wrought miracles.

Fabien tonight was wandering over the vast splendour of a sea of clouds, but below him lay eternity. He was lost among the constellations whose only denizen he was. He still held the world in his hands and balanced it against his chest. In his wheel he gripped the weight of human riches, and from one star to the next he was desperately peddling a useless treasure he would soon be made to yield.

A radio station was still listening to him, Rivière reflected. A faint melodic beat, a modulation in the minor key was all that now linked Fabien to the world. Not a plaint, not a cry. Only the purest sound despair has ever formed.

XIX

Robineau roused him from his loneliness.

"Monsieur le Directeur, I've been thinking . . . we could perhaps try . . ."

He had nothing to propose but thus proclaimed his good intentions. He would have so liked to come up with a solution, and he still sought one worriedly, like an answer to a conundrum. He always came up with solutions which Rivière never heeded. "In life, Robineau, there are no solutions. There are forces on the move, forces one must set in motion, and then the solutions follow." Robineau thus limited his role to setting up a motive force in the corps of the mechanics: a humble motive force which kept the propeller-bosses from rusting.

But the events of this night were more than Robineau could cope with. His title of inspector made no impression on the storms, nor on a phantom crew which was no longer battling for a punctuality bonus but to evade that dire penalty which nullified all of Robineau's—death. Now become superfluous, Robineau wandered aimlessly through the offices.

*

Fabien's wife had herself announced. Tormented by anxiety, she waited in the secretaries' office till Rivière could receive her. The secretaries shot stealthy glances at her face. It filled her with a kind of shame and she looked around with fright. Everything here was hostile to her. These men continuing their work as though they were trampling on a corpse, those files on which human life and suffering left no more than a residue of heartless figures. At home everything bespoke his absence: the rumpled bed, the coffee tray, a bouquet of flowers. But here ... there was not a sign, not a token. Everything warred with pity, friendship, remembrance. The only phrase she caught—for in her presence everyone spoke in undertones—was an oath uttered by an employee who had been demanding an invoice: "The invoice for the dynamos, for God's sake! The ones we sent to Santos." She looked at the man with an expression of utter bewilderment, and then at the wall, covered by a map. Her lips trembled slightly, almost imperceptibly.

She realized with embarrassment that here she represented an alien truth. She almost regretted having come, would have liked to hide, and for fear of attracting too much attention, restrained herself from coughing or crying. She felt out of place, indecent, as though naked. Yet so forceful was her truth that the furtive glances kept returning, unseen, to read the expression on her face. She was a woman of unusual beauty. She was the living revelation of the sacred world of happiness. She was the living revelation of the august matter one unwittingly tampers with when one acts. Disconcerted by so many curious glances, she closed her eyes, revealing the peace one can unwittingly destroy.

Rivière received her.

She had come to make a timid plea on behalf of her flowers, her waiting coffee, her young flesh. In this office, which was even colder than the others, her lips once again began to tremble faintly. She too now discovered her own truth in this other, alien world. The almost savage, fervent, devoted quality of her love here seemed to her to assume an egotistical, an importunate guise. She would have liked to flee.

"I am disturbing you . . ."

"Madame," Rivière said to her, "you are not disturbing me. Unfortunately, Madame, you and I can do nothing more than wait."

There was a faint tremor in her shoulders. Rivière guessed its meaning: "What's the point of that lamp, that waiting supper, the flowers I'll be going back to?" A young mother had one day confessed to Rivière: "The death of my child is something I still haven't understood. It's the tiny things that are hard, his little baby clothes I keep finding, and when I wake up at night that wave of tenderness which rises in my heart, in spite of everything, and which is now so useless, like my milk . . ." For this woman too Fabien's death would not really begin until tomorrow—in each act, each object, henceforth vain. Rivière had to hide the deep pity he felt for her.

"Madame . . ."

The young woman withdrew, with an almost humble smile, unconscious of her power.

Rivière sat down heavily.

"Still, she's helped me discover what I was looking for . . ."

Absent-mindedly he fingered the weather reports which had come in from the northern airfields. "We don't ask to be eternal," he thought. "What we ask is not to see acts and objects abruptly lose their meaning. The void surrounding us then suddenly yawns on every side."

His eyes strayed back to the telegrams. "And this is how death creeps into our affairs—through these messages, now bereft of meaning . . ."

He looked at Robineau. That middling fellow had also lost his meaning and was useless. Rivière addressed him almost gruffly:

"Must I be the one to find things for you to do?"

Rivière pushed through the door leading into the secretaries' office. He was struck by certain tell-tale signs Madame Fabien had been unable to detect. A slip marked R.B. 903—the number of Fabien's plane—was already tacked up on the wall chart under the heading of "Unavailable Materiel". The secretaries who were preparing the clearance papers for the Europe-bound mail were working slackly, knowing that its departure would be delayed. The airfield was ringing through for instructions to give the crews who now found themselves on night duty with nothing to do. The pace of life was slowing down. "Death, there it is!" thought Rivière. His work was now becalmed, like a stricken sailing vessel on a windless sea.

He heard Robineau's voice: "Monsieur le Directeur . . . they'd been married just six weeks."

"Get on with your work," said Rivière, pulling out his watch. Looking at the secretaries, he thought of the mechanics, the groundcrews, the pilots, of all those who had helped him in his task with a faith of builders. He thought of the little ports of long ago which having heard speak of magic "Isles", set to work to build a ship. A ship to be freighted with their hopes, whose sails would one day fill with the breath of their dreams as it headed out to sea. Thanks to a ship all of them were aggrandized, all delivered of themselves. "The end perhaps justifies nothing, but action delivers man from death. These men lasted by virtue of their ship."

Rivière too would be struggling against death, once he could restore full meaning to these telegrams, anxiety to the crews on duty, and a dramatic goal to his pilots. Once the breath of life revived this enterprise, as the wind revives a sail-boat on the sea.

XX

Comodoro Rivadavia could now hear nothing; but twenty minutes later and six hundred miles to the north, Bahía Blanca picked up a second message:

"Beginning descent. Entering clouds . . ."

Then these two words from a blurred message were intercepted by the radio station at Trelew:

". . . see nothing . . ."

Short-wave transmissions are like that. They are picked up in one place but elsewhere one hears nothing. Then, for no apparent reason, everything is changed. A plane, whose position is unknown, suddenly manifests itself to the world of the living, out of time and space, and the words that show up on the empty pads of radio stations are already those of phantoms.

Was the fuel supply exhausted, or was the pilot playing his last card before his engine failed—trying to make contact with the ground without crashing?

"Put the question to him," Buenos Aires ordered Trelew.

*

The radio station looks a bit like a laboratory—with its nickel and copper strips, its tuners and its sheaves of wires. In their white overalls the radio operators seem silently bent over a simple experiment. With their delicate fingers they manipulate the instruments, explore the magnetic sky, diviners probing for the vein of gold.

"No answer?"

"No answer."

Perhaps they will catch this note which would be a sign of life. If the plane and its wing-lights rise up among the stars, they may perhaps hear the song of this errant star.

The seconds ooze by. They really ooze like blood. Are they still in the air, or is their flight ended? Each second slays a hope. The flow of time now seems destructive. Twenty centuries of wear and tear, beating against the temple, nibbling and fissuring the granite and finally reducing it to dust, are now concentrated into each second threatening the crew.

Each second carries something away—Fabien's voice, Fabien's laugh, his smile. The silence gains ground. A heavier and heavier silence, bearing down on this crew like the weight of the sea.

"It's 1.40," someone finally observes. "The extreme limit of their fuel. They can't be flying any more."

Now all is calm. The watchers are left with a bitter taste in the mouth, like that of a journey's end. Something mysterious has come to pass, something a bit sickening. In the midst of all these nickeled plates and copper arteries one experiences the gloom that reigns over ruined factories. All this materiel seems ponderous, useless, unemployed, a weight of dead branches.

One can only wait for daylight.

In a few hours all of Argentina will emerge into the daylight, and these men will be there still, like fishermen on the strand, watching the net that is being slowly, oh so slowly dragged in, and without their knowing what it will contain.

*

In his office Rivière now felt the *détente* which comes in the aftermath of great disasters, when man is released from fate's uncertainty. He had alerted the police of an entire province. He could do no more, he could only wait. But order must reign even in the house of the dead.

Rivière beckoned to Robineau:

"Get this message off to the northern airfields: 'Anticipate serious delay Patagonia mail-plane. To avoid undue delay Europe mail, will add Patagonia to next Europe mail.' "

Feeling a jab of pain, he bent forward a little. Then, with an effort, he remembered something, something serious. Ah yes! Lest he forget it he called: "Robineau!"

"Monsieur Rivière?"

"You will draft a memo. Pilots are forbidden to exceed 1,900 r.p.m. They're wrecking the engines."

"Very well, Monsieur Rivière."

Rivière bowed his head, a little further. Solitude, above all, was what he needed.

"That's all, Robineau. You can run along, old man . . ."

And Robineau felt almost frightened at this equality before the dark unknown.

XXI

Robineau now wandered sadly through the offices. The life of the Company was at a standstill; for the Europe-bound mail, due to leave at 2 a.m., would now not leave before dawn. The employees sat morosely by their desks, frozen-faced now that their vigil was pointless. From the northern airfields the weather reports kept coming in at a steady pace; but their "clear skies", "full moon", and "no wind" evoked the image of a lifeless kingdom. A desert of moonlight and stones.

As Robineau, for no particular reason, began

leafing through a file the head clerk had been working on, he suddenly realized that the latter was
standing in front of him, waiting with an air of
mocking deference to get it back. The expression on
his face seemed to say: "When it pleases you, you
know . . . It's mine . . ."

The inspector felt shocked by this attitude on the
part of a subordinate, but unable to think of a retort,
he handed the file brusquely back. The head clerk
resumed his seat with an air of grave superiority. "I
should have sent him packing," thought Robineau.
To regain face he walked on, his thoughts focused
on the crisis. This crisis would entail the abandon-
ment of a policy, and Robineau felt a sense of two-
fold loss.

He was assailed by the vision of Rivière, alone
there in his office, Rivière who had said to him ". . .
old man". Never had someone so lacked support as
he. Robineau felt a floodtide of compassion go out
towards him. In his mind he turned over a number
of phrases vaguely aimed to express sympathy and
consolation. He was moved by a feeling which struck
him as quite noble.

He now knocked gently on the door. There was
no answer. Not daring to knock more loudly in the
prevailing silence, he pushed open the door. Rivière
was there. For the first time Robineau entered
Rivière's office almost on an equal footing, a bit like
a friend. He felt a bit like the sergeant who joins
the wounded general under fire, stands by him in
defeat, and behaves like a brother to him in exile.

"Whatever happens, I am with you," Robineau seemed to say.

Rivière spoke not a word; his head somewhat bowed, he was looking at his hands. Robineau, standing before him, dared not speak. Even stricken, the old lion daunted him. Expressions of loyalty, of ever more rapt devotion kept mounting to his lips, but each time he raised his eyes he encountered the grey hair, the head three-quarters bowed, the lips tight-sealed over their bitter potion. Finally he screwed up his courage:

"Monsieur le Directeur . . ."

Rivière raised his head and looked at him. The reverie into which Rivière had been plunged was so deep, so distant that he may not yet have noticed Robineau's presence. Nor could anyone know what it was he had been dreaming, feeling, and mourning in his heart. Rivière looked at Robineau for a long instant as a living witness to something. Robineau felt ill at ease. The longer Rivière looked at Robineau, the more it seemed as if a smile of enigmatic irony was playing about the former's lips. The longer Rivière looked at Robineau, the deeper Robineau blushed and the more it seemed to Rivière that Robineau had come, with a touching and regrettably spontaneous good-will, to bear witness to the foolishness of human beings.

Robineau felt increasingly dismayed. The sergeant, the general, the bullets all now seemed grotesquely out of place. A puzzling transformation came over him. Rivière was still looking at him.

Robineau, almost despite himself, straightened up a bit and took his hand out of his left pocket. Rivière still looked at him. Whereupon, feeling an intense embarrassment and not quite knowing why, Robineau blurted out:

"I have come to receive your orders."

Rivière pulled out his watch and said in the simplest of tones: "It's 2 o'clock. The mail-plane from Asunción will land at 2.10. Have the Europe-bound mail-plane take off at 2.15."

Robineau went out to propagate the astounding news: the night flights were not being interrupted.

"Bring me that file of yours to check," said Robineau to the chief clerk.

"Wait!" he said when the chief clerk was in front of him.

And the chief clerk waited.

XXII

The mail-plane from Asunción signalled that it was about to land. Even during the most critical moments Rivière had followed its successful progress telegram by telegram. In the midst of the débâcle this was his revenge, the living proof of his faith. This successful flight augured a thousand others that would be equally successful. "We don't get a cyclone every night," thought Rivière. "And once the trail is blazed, there is nothing for it but to continue."

Descending, airfield by airfield, from Paraguay, as though from an enchanted garden filled with flowers, pavilions, and slow waters, the plane had skirted the edge of a cyclone which had failed to dim a single star. Wrapped in their travelling rugs, the nine passengers pressed their foreheads to the panes, as though before a shop window full of gems: already the towns of Argentina were stringing their gold beads across the night, beneath the paler gold of the cities of stars above. Up front the pilot held his precious cargo of human lives in his hands, his wide-open eyes filled with moonlight, like a goatherd. The horizon already glowed with the rosy fire of Buenos Aires, and soon, like a fabled treasure, it would flaunt its diadem of jewels. The radio operator was tapping out the final telegrams, like the last notes of a sonata gaily tinkled in the sky for Rivière's enjoyment. Then he pulled in the aerial, stretched himself a bit, yawned, and smiled. The trip was over.

The pilot, after landing, found the pilot of the Europe-bound mail leaning against his plane with his hands in his pockets.

"You're flying the next hop?"

"Yes."

"Is the Patagonia in?"

"We're not waiting for it. It's disappeared. Good weather?"

"Weather's fine. You mean Fabien's disappeared?"

They said little; for a deep sense of brotherhood made extra phrases unnecessary.

While the mailbags from Asunción were being transferred to the Europe-bound plane, the pilot, leaning back against the fuselage, stood there motionless, gazing up at the stars. He felt a mighty power stirring within him, and it filled him with a potent joy.

"All loaded?" a voice asked. "O.K. Contact!"

The pilot did not budge, as his engine was started. Leaning back against the plane with his shoulders, he could feel the plane begin to live. Now at last, after so many false alarms—will leave . . . won't leave . . . will leave—the pilot would know for sure. His lips parted and his teeth glistened under the moon like a lion cub's.

"Watch out! The night, eh . . ."

He didn't hear his companion's advice. His hands in his pockets, his head thrown back, he thought of the clouds and the mountains, the rivers and the seas, and he broke into a silent laugh. A faint laugh which ran through him, like a breeze through a tree, and which thrilled him to the core. A faint laugh, but so much stronger than those clouds and mountains, those seas and rivers.

"Say, what's tickling you?"

"That fool Rivière who told me . . . who seems to think I'm scared!"

XXIII

In a minute he would be flying over Buenos Aires, and Rivière, who had resumed the struggle, wanted to hear him. Hear him murmur, roar, and die away, like the mighty tramp of an army marching through the stars.

His arms folded, Rivière passed among his secretaries. He paused behind a window and listened thoughtfully. If he had held up even one departure, his battle on behalf of night flights would have been lost. But to forestall the craven-hearted who tomorrow would disown him, Rivière had launched this other crew into the night.

Victory . . . defeat . . . these words are meaningless. Life lies deeper than these images, and is already at work, preparing new ones. A victory weakens one nation, defeat arouses another. The defeat Rivière had suffered was perhaps the commitment needed to spur on the decisive victory. For what mattered was the onward movement, the momentum.

In five minutes the radio stations would have alerted the airfields, and over ten thousand miles the quickening pulse of life would be resolving all problems.

Already a deep organ note was swelling—the plane.

And Rivière returned to his work, walking slowly past the secretaries cowed by his stern gaze. Rivière the Great, Rivière the Triumphant, bearing his heavy burden of victory.